THE RIVERSIDE MURDER

Rachel McLean writes thrillers that make your pulse race and your brain tick. Originally a self-publishing sensation, she has sold millions of copies digitally, with massive success in the UK, and a growing reach internationally. She is the author of the Dorset Crime novels and the spin-off McBride & Tanner series and Cumbria Crime series. In 2021, she won the Kindle Storyteller Award with *The Corfe Castle Murders* and her books regularly hit No1 in the Bookstat ebook chart on launch.

ALSO BY RACHEL MCLEAN

Dorset Crime series

The Corfe Castle Murders
The Clifftop Murders
The Island Murders
The Monument Murders
The Millionaire Murders
The Fossil Beach Murders
The Blue Pool Murders
The Lighthouse Murders
The Ghost Village Murders
The Poole Harbour Murders
...and more to come

RACHEL MCLEAN

DORSET CRIME SERIES NOVELLA

THE RIVERSIDE MURDER

ACKROYD PUBLISHING

Copyright © 2022 by Rachel McLean

All rights reserved.

No part of this book may be reproduced in any form or by any electronic or mechanical means, including information storage and retrieval systems, without written permission from the author, except for the use of brief quotations in a book review.

This is a work of fiction. Names, characters, businesses, places, events and incidents are either the products of the author's imagination or used in a fictitious manner. Any resemblance to actual persons, living or dead, or actual events is purely coincidental.

Ackroyd Publishing

ackroydpublishing.com

Printed and bound in the UK by CPI Group (Uk) Ltd, Croydon CR0 4YY

CHAPTER ONE

DCI Lesley Clarke had to focus to keep herself from tumbling down the hill towards the River Frome. This lane, a mile or so from Wareham in Dorset, was steep and narrow, the trees reaching over her head and meeting there like a green archway. Her second in command DS Dennis Frampton huffed along behind her, unhappy that they'd had to walk down.

"Come on, Dennis," she called back to him. "Gail's been there almost an hour. At this rate, even Whittaker will get there before us."

Gail Hansford was Lesley's favourite crime scene manager, which was lucky since most of the time she was the only crime scene manager available. The county of Dorset didn't have enough complex crimes to justify an army of forensic technicians. Henry Whittaker, by contrast, was her least favourite pathologist. She'd never yet known him arrive at a crime scene on time.

At last they emerged from the canopy of trees where the

road widened out, and stopped just short of the river, where it turned into a narrow footpath.

"Where are we going?" Lesley asked, turning back to Dennis. The sun was strong now they'd left the shelter of the woods, and she had to raise a hand to shield her eyes.

Dennis gestured upstream, where a rough track led alongside the river and towards what looked like a marina. "They found him on the sliproad, just before the marina."

Lesley nodded and carried on walking. Her work in Dorset Police had made her fit. The criminals were selfish here: they tended not to commit their crimes in a convenient spot with nearby parking. Lesley had learned early on that yomping across the countryside was part of the job description.

She turned a bend to see Gail and her team further along the river, struggling to erect a forensic tent in the shallows.

"You sure that'll work?" she called out.

Gail flinched and dropped the corner of the tent she'd been holding. One of her white-suited colleagues picked it up.

"Lesley!" she called. "You're SIO?"

"Who else have they got to choose from?" It wasn't as if Lesley's department had many DCIs who could act as senior investigating officer on a murder investigation.

"Good." Gail gestured for Lesley to follow her towards the spot where her two colleagues almost had the tent upright.

"First question," Lesley began. "Is there a crime for me to investigate?"

"We'll know more when the pathologist gets here," said Gail. "But I think so." She held open the flaps to the tent. "Signs of a struggle, see? Rocks dislodged, edge of the water."

Lesley looked down. "You want me to wade into the water?"

"It's shallow. I thought we should leave him where he is until the pathologist has seen him. Then we'll move him a bit further up the bank. Here."

Gail held out a pair of wellies and Lesley slid them on, leaning on her friend's shoulder.

"Right." She stepped into the tent and approached the body. It was face down in the water, the features hidden. But it was definitely a man. He was huge: six foot five if he was an inch. His shoulders were broad and his frame heavy but not fat. Lesley imagined it would be easy to identify him.

"Do we know who he is?"

"Not officially, but Gav here thinks it's William Coombs."

One of the white-suited techs lifted his face mask and gave Lesley a nod. "I'm pretty sure it's him, Ma'am."

"You don't have to ma'am me." Gavin was a civilian, and she was getting tired of having to remind him about this.

"Sorry."

"You know – knew him?"

Gavin nodded. "My brother drank with him at the Duke of Wellington. Haven't seen him for – oh, has to be more than a decade, though."

Lesley raised an eyebrow. It was possible her girlfriend Elsa might know the man too. She'd had a stint working in that pub, more recently, but you never knew.

"How long has he been here?"

"It's a busy Saturday afternoon. He was spotted by the couple who've bought the farmhouse up there." Gail gestured past the marina.

"You've given me his name, but who is he? Something to do with the marina?"

Gail shook her head. "He used to own the farm. Part-own. His brother was the one who farmed it."

"He sold it to the people who found him dead?" Lesley narrowed her eyes. Was that suspicious, or just a coincidence?

Gail shrugged. "Mr Dewsbury came down here to check out the area, find out what was on his doorstep. They only moved in yesterday."

Lesley opened the flap of the tent and looked back out, towards a boulder where a man in his forties sat, a uniformed police officer standing in front of him and taking notes.

"We'll need to speak to him." She leaned out of the tent. "Dennis, can you speak to the witness please?"

Dennis looked from her to the man and back again, a question on his face.

"He found the body," she told him. "Get a statement."

"Boss." Dennis hurried towards the man and Lesley let the fabric of the tent drop.

"Gavin," she said. "You knew the victim. Do you think there's anything fishy about him being discovered dead by the bloke who bought his farm?"

"Not the farm, Ma'am."

Lesley let the *ma'am* go. "How d'you mean?"

"The land was sold off in bits. Fred Vickery up towards Corfe got half of it, Andy Towns from over the other side of Wareham bought most of the rest. God knows why, but there you go. The new family just bought the building and the land around it. They're not local."

Lesley allowed herself a smile, wondering what the people of Wareham had thought about outsiders buying a farmhouse that might have stood here for centuries. "Either way, we'll need to talk to them. Did the deceased have family?"

"His brother."

"The farmer?"

"Yes. Former farmer."

"And where is he, now he's sold all his property and filled his bank account?"

"He's got a bungalow in Swanage."

"That must feel odd after years of farming."

"I heard his wife's ill. Mental health."

Lesley nodded. "We'll need to get a car round there. He's next of kin, by the sounds of it. I'll want to interview him and the rest of the family."

"Er..." Gavin gave her an awkward look.

"Lesley," Gail said. "Gav's a CSI. He can't tell Uniform to send a car."

Lesley shook her head. "No. You're right. Sorry, Gavin." She pushed open the door to the tent and approached Dennis, pulling her phone from her pocket.

CHAPTER TWO

LESLEY SAT in the passenger seat of Dennis's car as they drove away from Wareham and towards Corfe Castle, which lay between the crime scene and the bungalow in Swanage where the victim's brother lived.

"So, how many family members are we going to have to speak to?" she asked, enunciating clearly for the benefit of the rest of her team, who were listening through the hands-free function on the phone clamped to Dennis's dashboard.

"There's the brother," replied PC Tina Abbott from the office. "You know about him."

"Is there just one brother?" Dennis asked. "No other siblings?"

"Not that we know of, Sarge," Tina replied.

"He and his brother were the only sons?" Lesley asked. She knew that daughters could get passed over when it came to inheriting farms, especially back in the seventies or eighties, when she imagined this particular farm would last have changed hands.

CHAPTER TWO

"There was a girl, but she died," Tina said. "Drowned when she was six."

Dennis winced. "Poor mite."

Lesley scratched the back of her neck, a shiver running across her skin. "Could that be relevant?"

"The sister drowning as well?" Dennis asked.

"Whoever killed him might have been referencing that."

Dennis frowned. "It was years ago. Tina, when did the girl die?"

"Margaret Coombs. Born in 1949, died in 1955. I've found some press cuttings, it was a big deal at the time."

"I bet it was," Dennis muttered. He crossed himself, ever so quickly. Lesley raised an eyebrow but said nothing.

"OK," she said. "Tina, find out what you can about Margaret's death. And get names and addresses for all of the family."

"Boss," came a male voice over the phone. DC Johnny Chiles.

"Johnny," Lesley said. "What is it?"

"Er, the guy who's just died, William. He went missing twelve years ago, never found. Not as far as the file says, anyway."

"Twelve years ago?"

"Yes. Christmas time. His sister-in-law filed a missing persons report, looks like it wasn't given much attention, him being a fifty-odd year-old adult and all, but there's nothing on the record about him turning up again."

"Is the sister-in-law still living locally?"

"Swanage."

"With the brother."

"Her husband."

"OK," Lesley said. "So, what, he disappeared? Moved away, maybe? And now he's back, and dead."

"Maybe he turned up but they never told the police," Dennis suggested.

"Maybe," Johnny agreed.

"Still," Lesley added. "It's another angle. We'll ask the brother about it when we speak to him. Johnny and Tina, find out what you can about that missing persons case. Was any resource put into it, and is there any background on why he might have gone AWOL, assuming he really did?"

"No problem, boss."

"Good. Where's Mike?"

"He rang in sick," Johnny said.

"He's got some sort of bug," Tina added. "Food poisoning, maybe."

Lesley exchanged a grimace with Dennis. "Tell him to get better soon, Tina."

"Will do." There was a trace of embarrassment in Tina's voice. The team all knew that Tina and DC Mike Legg were an item, but they didn't really talk about it.

Lesley hung up. She stared out of the windscreen as Dennis drove. Clouds were gathering up ahead over the coast. She shivered.

"Right," she said. "Let's see how much his brother can fill in."

CHAPTER THREE

Norris Coombs lived in a squat bungalow on the edge of Swanage with a view of fields and distant glimpses of the sea between the neighbouring houses. Lesley pressed the doorbell and waited, Dennis shuffling between his feet next to her. It was starting to rain.

"Yes?" asked a thin, grey-haired man wearing a faded purple fleece as he opened the door.

Lesley glanced up and down the street. No sign of Uniform yet; they were going to have to break the news.

She held up her ID. "I'm DCI Clarke from Dorset Police. This is my colleague DS Frampton. Are you Norris Coombs?"

"I am. What's happened? It's not the farm, is it? I don't own it any—"

"It's not the farm, Mr Coombs. Can we come in?"

His expression fell. People knew what it meant when the police asked to come in: bad news. "Who?" he asked in a quiet voice.

Lesley sighed. No point in prolonging this. "Your

brother, William. He was found on the riverbank near Wareham this morning. I'm sorry to have to tell you this, but he drowned."

"William?" Coombs shook his head. "That's impossible."

"Impossible?" Dennis asked.

The man turned to him, his expression dismissive. "William died twelve years ago."

"We're aware he went missing," Lesley said. "You were told that he'd died?"

Norris had deflated. He leaned against the doorframe, suddenly small. "We assumed... You mean he's been in the area all along?"

"I'm afraid we don't know where he was in the intervening time, Mr Coombs. Can we come in and ask you a few questions?"

He glanced behind him. "My wife's asleep."

'We'll be quiet," Dennis said.

"No, it's not that. She gets... agitated if she wakes and there are strangers in the house." He swallowed. "Dementia."

"Sorry to hear that," said Dennis. "Would you rather come to the police station to talk to us, maybe later when your wife is awake?"

Norris looked alarmed. "No. God, no. I can't leave her." He looked behind him again. "Come in."

He held the door open and stood back for them to pass. People did this; they thought it was polite to let the police officers go first. But once they were inside, Lesley and Dennis had no idea where to go.

They waited in the hall while Norris closed the front door and went to the bottom of the stairs. He peered up for a moment, not speaking.

CHAPTER THREE

"Where would you like us?" Dennis asked, his voice barely more than a whisper.

"Through here." Norris gestured to a door, which Lesley opened. Beyond it was a comfortable living room. Sofas filled the space, taking up more room than they should have, and packing boxes were piled on an armchair. Norris pointed to a further set of doors leading through to a light-filled conservatory with views toward Ballard Down.

The conservatory was untidy, packing paper and tape scattered around a table and scuffed chairs.

"Sorry about the mess."

"Don't worry about us," Lesley said. She took a seat at the table and waited for Norris to do the same. "Can you tell us about your brother's disappearance?"

"When was he found?" Norris lowered himself into a chair, kicking a ball of packing tape away from his feet.

"Mid-morning today," Lesley told him. "The pathologist is at the scene now but it's safe to say he drowned."

"Is it suspicious?"

"Would you expect it to be?"

He eyed her for a few moments. "I know what you're doing."

Lesley said nothing.

"If I give you a reason why his death might be suspicious, you'll think I'm making it up. If I don't, you'll suspect me."

"I assure you, we aren't that devious," she told him. "We just want to find out more about your brother and what might have led to his death."

"You still haven't told me if it was suspicious. But I wouldn't expect a DCI and a DS on my doorstep within a matter of hours if it wasn't." He looked at Dennis, who shuffled in his chair.

Lesley leaned in. "Yes, Mr Coombs. There are signs that your brother might have been involved in a struggle before he died. It might be unrelated, but we have to work on the basis that someone may have assaulted him."

"Just assaulted?"

"The struggle and his drowning may or may not be related. We'll know more after the post-mortem. But I'm sure you'll understand that there are aspects of this that we can't talk about at this stage."

"Yes." Norris looked down at his hands, which were clasped together on the table. "I still don't understand what he was doing in Wareham, after so long." He looked up, his mouth falling open. "Which stretch of the river? I used to own a farm along the Frome."

Lesley nodded. "He was found about quarter of a mile from your former farm."

"Shit." Norris slumped in his chair. Dennis glanced up at Lesley and then quickly away again, and she fought to suppress a smile. "Is there evidence he was coming to see me?"

"He didn't make contact with you at all?" Dennis asked. "Nothing recent?"

"Nothing. I don't understand." He let out a thin breath. "God, if he was looking for me..." He wiped away a tear. "Poor bastard."

Dennis grunted. Lesley ignored it; Dennis didn't approve of blasphemy or bad language, but it wasn't his place to tell a man who'd just lost his brother how to react.

"Is there anyone else in the family he might have made contact with?" she asked. "Did he have a wife or partner?"

"No. William couldn't hold onto a girlfriend for more

CHAPTER THREE

than a few months. He drank, you see. Heavily. Used to practically live at the Duke of Wellington."

Lesley chewed her lip. The Duke of Wellington again. But that would have been long before Elsa worked there.

"Did he have any friends, drinking buddies maybe?" she asked. "Anyone he might have sought out if he was returning to the area?"

'You think he was returning? Not that he was here all along?"

"I'd imagine it would have been difficult for him to live here for twelve years without being recognised."

"Yes. I suppose you're right." Norris's voice was low.

There was a sound from beyond the conservatory doors, a low shriek. Dennis straightened in his chair and shot Lesley a worried look.

"That's Harriet. I'm sorry, I'll have to ask you to leave. If she finds you here..."

Lesley stood up, pulling her business card from her pocket. "Of course. I'm assuming you won't be wanting us to send a Family Liaison Officer?"

"No. Thank you."

She nodded. FLOs weren't just for support; they were the investigation's eyes and ears in the home of the deceased or their families. But in this case, with the man having been missing for twelve years, that might not be so important.

That was, assuming he *had* been missing for twelve years.

She handed him the card. "If you need support, call me. And if you think of anything that might be relevant. Especially if you're able to find out anything about your brother's whereabouts in the last twelve years."

"I don't imagine I'm going to find that out now."

"Sometimes when people discover that someone has

died, they feel they can share things that they couldn't before. If anything does come up, tell us. Please."

He sniffed. "Of course." Another wail came from upstairs. "Please, I am going to have to ask you to hurry."

He bundled them out of the house in silence, all the while glancing anxiously upstairs. Lesley wished they could get a moment with Mrs Coombs. Dementia or not, she might be able to remember details from twelve years ago that her husband could have dismissed or forgotten.

They stumbled out to the front drive, the door shutting quietly behind them.

"Rude," Lesley said.

"Odd, more like," Dennis replied.

"You think so?"

"How can his brother have been hanging around locally and he didn't know?"

"Well, he probably wasn't, was he? And William went to Norris's farm. He didn't even know his brother had moved."

"Still." Dennis raised an eyebrow. "It's not like you not to be suspicious, boss."

She gave him a smile. "Oh don't worry, Dennis. I'm plenty suspicious. Now let's get back to the office and see what they've got for us."

CHAPTER FOUR

Tina had already cleared the last case off the whiteboard in Lesley's office, and stuck up photos of the latest crime scene and victim. Hand-drawn lines led to images of Norris and Harriet Coombs, and two younger women as well as a young man.

"Who are they?" Lesley asked as she sat down behind her desk. The team, or those of them who weren't off sick, were all present: Dennis standing by the door almost as if to attention, Johnny lounging in a chair, Tina at the board.

Tina pointed to the images one by one with her marker pen. "Ruth and Amanda Coombs. Norris and Harriet's daughters."

"And the other one?" Dennis asked.

"Tom Gains. William's son."

"I thought he didn't have a family?" Lesley asked.

"Illegitimate. Unacknowledged, from what I can tell. When William went missing, he wasn't around. No mention of him in the files. But then two months later he turned up and tried to get them to reopen the investigation into his father's disappearance."

"Why wasn't he around earlier?" Johnny asked.

"Good question," added Lesley. "Any idea?"

"The notes don't go into that kind of detail, boss," Tina told her. "It's all on paper, I haven't been able to check all of it."

Lesley sniffed. "OK, you and Johnny need to prioritise that. I want to know what the history was. Why wasn't Tom Gains in the area when his dad went missing, and why did he suddenly turn up? What was the relationship between them like? Was Tom under suspicion at any point?"

"I think they just reckoned William had decided to up sticks," Johnny said.

"But William had a drinking habit," Dennis pointed out. "He could have got into trouble. The investigating team might have assumed he'd got drunk and managed to fall in the sea or something." He wrinkled his nose, and Lesley wondered whether Dennis might be teetotal. It wouldn't surprise her.

"He clearly didn't do that, though," she said. "Given that he's turned up dead twelve years later."

Dennis shrugged.

"OK," she said. "Tina, Johnny. Continue with the files. And let me know when we get the full pathologist's report. I'm not ruling out this being an accidental death after all."

"But won't—?" Tina began.

"Until we get the full report, we can't assume anything. Even if William wasn't murdered, I'd like to know why he vanished for so long. That in itself could be suspicious."

"Yes, boss."

"Thanks." Lesley stood up. "OK, let's get on with it."

CHAPTER FIVE

"D'you want me to drive this time?" Lesley asked Dennis as they left Dorset Police headquarters in Winfrith. It was an ugly modern building that looked a lot like a motorway service station.

"It's fine, boss. I know the roads better."

"Oi. I've been here long enough to know where I'm going. And besides, have you heard of a little thing called satnav?"

Dennis smiled, not meeting her eye. He never used satnav, instead relying on his encyclopaedic knowledge of the Dorset roads. If they ever devised a version of the London taxi driver's Knowledge for Dorset, Dennis would breeze through it.

Lesley slid into the passenger seat and rearranged her thoughts as Dennis backed out of the parking space. He'd parked on the opposite side of the car park from the building again. His wife Pam had him on a health kick, and he reckoned this helped him get his steps in. Lesley would rather get to an interview quickly than worry about steps.

As they left the road, snaking around the police headquarters and joining the A352 through Wool, her phone rang. It was her girlfriend, Elsa.

"Hey sweetie," she said. "How's it going?"

"Deathly dull. Remind me to get one of the junior partners to sign up for Tort law courses instead of me next time, yes?"

"I still don't see why you're there. You're a criminal lawyer."

"Someone had to, and it doesn't do any harm to keep up your knowledge on other areas of the law. You never know when a client might need it."

"Sorry it's dull. You're back tomorrow?"

"Yes. I'm going to try and duck out after lunch. Will you be at the flat?"

Elsa had a flat in Bournemouth, three streets back from the seafront. Lesley officially lived in a cottage in Wareham that Dorset police had rented for the duration of her secondment, but she hated the place.

"Sorry. Murder case."

"Anything I need to know about?"

"There isn't a suspect yet."

"And they might not hire my firm even if there is."

"Exactly." Lesley and Elsa had faced each other across the interview table enough times; Lesley didn't want to encourage it.

"We're here," Dennis said.

"Elsa, have you heard of a William Coombs?"

"Sorry. No."

"Coombs family?"

"No."

"That's something in their favour, then. Got to go."

CHAPTER FIVE

Lesley blew a kiss down the line and hung up. Dennis raised an eyebrow and she pulled a face at him.

Their first port of call was at the home of Ruth, Norris Coombs's eldest daughter. She lived in a Victorian town house in Wareham. It was spick and span, flower boxes at the windows and the front path swept to within an inch of its life. A squad car was parked outside. So they wouldn't be breaking the news.

Dennis rapped the knocker– ornate, shiny, brass – and stood back. Lesley pulled on a sympathetic smile as a woman in her fifties opened the door. Her face was blotchy, her eyes rimmed with red.

She held up her ID. "I'm DCI Clarke, this is DS Frampton. You're Ruth Coombs?"

She nodded, wordless.

"Sorry to trouble you. I assume our colleagues in Uniform are already here?"

Another nod. The woman stood back and ushered them inside. In the kitchen, two uniformed officers sat at the table, looking uneasy. One of them was Simon Mullins, Tina's partner when she'd been on the beat.

"Ma'am. Sarge," they both muttered.

"Constables," Lesley replied. "D'you mind waiting outside?"

They exchanged relieved glances and headed out. Two burly men faced with a highly emotional older woman; they would be glad to leave it to her and Dennis.

She gave Ruth a smile and gestured towards the table. "Can we...?"

Another nod, and a sniff. Lesley looked at Dennis, who had raised that eyebrow again. She wondered if they were going to get anything useful out of this woman.

"I know this is difficult right now, but I'm sure you'll understand we want to work as quickly as we can to uncover the circumstances of your uncle's death."

Another nod. The woman slid into a chair and placed her hands on the table, palms down. Her knuckles were white.

"He was already dead," she muttered. "We'd grieved. This isn't..." She dragged a hanky out of her pocket and blew her nose.

"Your uncle disappeared twelve years ago, is that right?"

A nod.

"And you assumed he was dead?"

"It took four years for them to declare him dead. It was..."

Lesley waited.

"It was what?" she asked.

Ruth gave her a hard look. "It was difficult."

"I can imagine," Dennis said. "Not being able to achieve closure—"

"No." The woman jerked her head towards him. "It wasn't that."

"What *was* it?" Lesley was still recovering from her surprise at hearing Dennis use the word *closure*. "Did something else happen, as well as your uncle's disappearance?"

Ruth Coombs dragged her hands across the table, her nails scraping on the wood. "You could say that." She stood up. Lesley watched as she went to the sink and ran it. She splashed water on her face and turned back towards them.

"You may as well know. Everyone else bloody did."

Lesley nodded, waiting.

Ruth approached the table again. She gripped the back of her chair. "My mum. She told him."

"Told who? Your uncle?"

A shake of the head. "My dad. Well, that's what he..."

CHAPTER FIVE

She drew in a breath, her chest rising. "William was my dad, you see. My real dad."

Lesley kept her eyes on the woman. This would have been shocking news to Ruth, but to a seasoned DCI, it was just a possible lead. "William was your father."

"There was a row. Before William went missing. My mum let it out. They thought I wasn't there, but I'd come to visit and just opened the door when I heard it. If I'd turned up five minutes later, I'd still be none the wiser."

"So you think William's disappearance had something to do with that?"

A shrug. "No one would talk to me about it. It was like the whole thing never happened. I sometimes wonder about him and my mum..."

Lesley frowned. "In what way?"

Ruth eyed her. "Nothing."

Lesley looked back at the woman. "Did your father, Norris I mean, did he ever hurt you?"

Ruth frowned. "No. Of course not."

"Did he hurt your mum?"

Ruth gripped the chair tighter. "I can't be sure. There were times when she... bruises, scratches, things she dismissed as having happened on the farm. She said it was nothing."

Lesley swallowed. "Ruth, do you think Norris might have killed William?"

Silence. Lesley watched the woman's face twist through a variety of emotions. Finally she looked Lesley in the eye for the first time.

"Yes," she said. "Yes, I think he might have."

CHAPTER SIX

"So," said Dennis as they drove out of Wareham towards Corfe Castle, "you think it's that simple?"

She shook her head. "I wouldn't like to make any assumptions just yet."

Her phone rang: Henry Whittaker, the curmudgeonly pathologist.

"Dr Whittaker," she said. "Have you got news?"

"The body is at the morgue but we don't have the capacity to do a PM today."

She gritted her teeth. *Bloody Whittaker*. "It's a suspicious death. I want to know if it was murder before I waste police resources on—"

"I know, DCI Clarke. Urgent case. They're always urgent. But we have finite resources, you know."

Lesley sighed. She should consider herself lucky that Whittaker had even come out to the crime scene. "When will you be able to do it, Henry?"

She knew he would hate the *Henry*.

"Tomorrow morning. First thing."

CHAPTER SIX

That was as good as she was going to get. "Good. I'll send someone along. Do you have anything else for me in the meantime?"

"There was an object in his throat."

"An object?"

Dennis turned to her, taking his eyes from the road for a moment. He caught himself and turned back, his hands firm on the steering wheel.

"What kind of object?" she asked.

"A thimble."

She thumped her knee, making Dennis jerk.

"A thimble? You found a thimble in his throat and you think there's even the slightest chance someone didn't do this to him?"

"DCI Clarke, please. People do strange things. I haven't found evidence of the object being forced into his throat. There are no bruises internally, no lacerations. There's just the disturbance of the ground around him that the CSIs are on about, but that might be nothing. You would—"

"Henry," she said. "Send me a photo of this bloody thimble, will you?"

Dennis sniffed. "Boss..."

"Sorry, Dennis. But this is an extreme situation."

Dennis didn't like her swearing. When she'd arrived on the team, he'd presented his swear box to her on multiple occasions. They'd come to a compromise that involved her toning down her language and him putting the box in a filing cabinet.

"Just send me the photo, Dr Whittaker," she snapped. "Or get the CSIs to." She hung up.

"A thimble?" Dennis asked. "Where?"

"In his throat."

Dennis's jaw hung open. Lesley smiled. "Be careful, something might fly in."

He pursed his lips then turned onto the B3351 towards Studland, where Norris Coombs's second daughter lived. His only daughter, really. They hadn't found an address for William's son yet.

"Someone put it there, surely," he said as they drove up the hill away from Corfe Castle.

"Whittaker says there's no sign of it being forced into his throat."

"But it wouldn't have just slid in. I mean, you don't find thimbles floating in the River Frome."

"No. It's certainly suspicious, whatever Whittaker says."

"I assume Gail Hansford is examining it for forensics."

"That's my next call."

Dennis nodded and leaned forward in his seat, taking the bends faster than Lesley had seen him do before. She picked up her phone.

"Lesley," Gail said as she answered the call. "You'll be calling me about this foreign object found in William Coombs's throat."

"The thimble."

"I'm doing the usual tests on it. Prints, DNA. Attempting to find out where it came from in the first place. But getting prints off something so small after it's been in the river, not to mention inside a body, is tricky. And even if I do, who's to say they're not just there because someone used the thimble for sewing?"

"And the same applies to DNA," Lesley said.

"Yes. But I'll see what I can get. The DNA could take a day or two."

Lesley stretched her neck. Pain from the injury she'd

sustained in her last job was still troubling her. "Keep me posted, will you Gail?"

"Of course."

Lesley rubbed her eyes as they approached Studland, It was getting dark, the houses difficult to differentiate in the village. At last Dennis pulled up outside a low cottage with a thatched roof that looked as if it had seen better days. Lesley silently congratulated herself on spotting the roof's sorry state; she was becoming a country girl, after all.

Dennis got out of the car and waited, cocking his head as she climbed out of the passenger seat.

"Everything OK, boss?"

"Fine." She put a hand to her neck. "Fine." At least the psychological effects were no longer troubling her.

"Would you like me to lead on this one?"

She frowned at him. "Thanks Dennis, but no. I'm fine." She walked ahead of him and rang the doorbell.

A thin man in his sixties answered. His face fell as he saw them. "Oh. Detectives, I suppose?"

Lesley nodded as she held up her ID. "I'm sorry to bother you. Is Amanda Coombs in?"

"Amanda Lloyd. That's my wife. Yes, she's in the living room. Be gentle with her, will you? It's been a shock."

Lesley smiled at him. "I'm sure it has." She wasn't making any promises, though. If the members of this family knew more about William's death than they were letting on, she'd get to the bottom of it.

He turned and walked along a narrow hallway. Pictures hung on the wall, as well as brass plaques. Brass figures of dogs and horses, medals from country shows. Lesley hadn't become so ingrained in local life that she had the first clue what they were.

"Boss." Dennis brushed her arm.

She turned to him. "What?"

He looked at her, and then at a point beyond her, his expression meaningful.

Lesley turned. On a narrow shelf was a row of thimbles. All of them were different: engraved, irregularly shaped. They were evenly spaced apart.

All, that was, except for two of them. Two of them had a gap between them that was twice as wide as the others.

Lesley was aware of Dennis holding his breath behind her. One of the thimbles was missing.

CHAPTER SEVEN

Amanda wasn't as emotional as her sister. Instead, she was cold and still. Lesley had the impression she was hiding something.

They'd asked her about family history and Amanda had given much the same story as her sister, albeit second-hand. It seemed the two women confided in each other.

"Did your uncle know he was your sister's real father?" Lesley asked.

"I have no idea."

"But your father did."

"Yes. You've heard about the argument."

"Mrs Lloyd, I know this is a sensitive question. But is there any chance William was also *your* father?"

Amanda straightened in her threadbare armchair. "Absolutely not." She looked between Lesley and Dennis. "Wait."

She stood up, strode out of the room and left them alone. Lesley gestured at Dennis, and he rose from his chair and strolled around the room. He peered into bookcases and checked shelves.

The door opened and Dennis slid back into his chair. Amanda gave him a disapproving look and he blushed. Lesley rolled her eyes.

The woman was holding a photo album. She opened it and flipped through the pages. "Here," she said.

She all but threw it into Lesley's lap, open at a photograph of a man in his thirties and a girl aged around ten.

"See?" she said. "Tell me that man isn't that girl's father."

She had a point. The two of them had the same thin lips, the same high cheeks.

Amanda grabbed the album and flicked through it again. She held it open at another photograph: a family snap taken at a wedding.

She pointed to the two men pictured, each in turn. Then she pointed at the two girls. "Me and my dad. Ruth and William. I think it's pretty clear, don't you?"

Even so, the two men were brothers. "Did you ever ask your mum if William might be your father?" Lesley asked.

Amanda pulled the album back towards her and gave Lesley a horrified look. "Good God no. I wasn't about to make things worse than they already were."

Lesley nodded. "Can I ask you about the collection of thimbles on the shelf in your hall?"

Amanda frowned. "Thimbles? What have they got to do with any of this?"

"There's one missing," Dennis said.

She turned to him. "Of course there isn't."

Lesley stood up and gestured for the woman to follow her. They walked out of the living room and into the hallway, where Lesley pointed to the thimble collection.

Amanda looked past her. "What are you talking about?"

Lesley turned towards the shelf. "There's one missing."

"No there isn't."

Lesley leaned in. It was dark in this space, the only light a dim table lamp by the front door.

The woman was right. The big gap she thought she'd seen wasn't there. Lesley counted the thimbles: ten. How many had there been before? She couldn't remember.

She turned to Dennis. "You saw it too, right?"

"Yes." He pointed to the spot where the gap had been. "There was one missing, there."

Amanda tutted. "Well I don't know what you're talking about. There's clearly no gap."

CHAPTER EIGHT

"There was a gap," Lesley said as they drove away from the house.

"There was," Dennis agreed. It was fully dark now, the beams of his headlights washing over the hedgerows as they drove and forming a tunnel of light.

"I don't suppose you made a note of how many there were?"

"There were ten."

"I know that."

"No," he replied. "I mean there were ten to start with. It wasn't that the missing one was put back. Someone had just rearranged the remaining ten."

"So they were hiding the fact that one was missing."

"We'll never prove it."

"We will if we can get prints or DNA off it."

Dennis nodded. He leaned towards the windscreen, his brow furrowed.

"You want me to take over?" Lesley asked.

CHAPTER EIGHT

"I'm fine. I wasn't expecting it to be this dark."

"You need to get home to your wife. We aren't going to get anything else useful tonight." She was glad Elsa was away, so she didn't have to feel guilty. But Elsa was a criminal lawyer, and she knew what long hours were.

"She said that no one had been in that hallway except for her and her husband," Lesley said.

"Not in the last week."

They'd questioned Amanda about the thimbles, trying not to reveal just how important they might be. It was the kind of crime scene detail it was best not to reveal. Relatives could be traumatised by that kind of thing, if they didn't know about it already. But the fact that someone in that house had tried to hide the gap among the thimbles suggested that they might well do.

"It was her mum's collection," Dennis said. "Harriet's."

"Harriet has dementia."

"That's what her husband told us."

Lesley turned to him. "You're right. We believed him." She thumped her forehead. "Why was I so credulous?"

"You had no reason not to be, boss. And Gav mentioned it too, at the scene."

"Still. Gav probably heard it from the same source we did. Norris Coombs."

They were almost back at the office. "I'll see you in the morning, Dennis. I just hope Tina and Johnny aren't still here." She realised she hadn't called and told them to go home. During a murder investigation, Tina in particular would work until she was told not to. Johnny, on the other hand, would head home as soon as it was suggested. But he was perceptive from time to time, and good with witnesses.

"It's OK," Dennis said. "I spoke to them when we left Ruth Coombs's house."

"Thanks. See you in the morning."

CHAPTER NINE

THE NEXT MORNING, Tina was already in when Lesley arrived. As she headed into her office, Dennis came into the main team room carrying two mugs.

"Morning, boss. Can I get you a coffee?"

"Please." She fished in her bag for some change. "Get me a Twix from the machine as well, will you? I didn't have breakfast."

He took the pound coin she held out and left the room.

"So Tina," she said. "No sign of Johnny yet?"

Tina shrugged. Johnny had a habit of turning up late.

"How's Mike?"

"Getting there." Tina tugged at her collar. "He phoned me this morning. Thinks he'll be back tomorrow."

Lesley knew damn well that Mike hadn't phoned Tina this morning, but she wasn't about to pierce the younger woman's privacy. "Good. Give him my best."

"Thanks."

Dennis reappeared with a mug of coffee and a Twix.

"Thanks." Lesley unwrapped it and bit off half of one

stick. She plunged the rest into her pocket. "So, what have we got? Tina, did you come up with any more history?"

Tina nodded and jerked her head towards Lesley's office, where the board was. Lesley noticed that Tina had placed it so its front was facing the wall. She approved: this office was too open-plan and she didn't like the idea that anyone passing might be able to see everything they were working on.

"Go on," Lesley said. Tina walked into the office, and Lesley and Dennis followed. As they entered, the outer door opened and Johnny appeared, his hair dishevelled.

They all turned and looked at him. He stared back at them.

"Am I late? Sorry."

Lesley grunted. Dennis checked his watch. "Three minutes, Johnny."

"Sorry, Sarge. Traffic."

Johnny was going to get himself reprimanded if he carried on like this. They all knew that Winfrith didn't have traffic.

"You're in luck, we haven't started yet," Lesley told him.

"Boss." He shuffled into her office, not meeting her eye. She shook her head. *If you're going to be late, at least be confident about it.*

She perched on the edge of the desk and gestured for Johnny and Dennis to take the two chairs that sat opposite it. Tina went to the board. Johnny lifted himself out of his chair, then Tina waved him back into it. He sat, looking uncomfortable.

"Tina," Lesley said. "Tell us what you and Johnny were able to find out."

Tina held onto the edge of the board. "William Coombs went missing twelve and a half years ago. There was an investigation that lasted two weeks, but when he didn't turn up, it was assumed he'd just left the county. I found a note in the file about a family argument, but it doesn't say what it was about."

"His daughter," Dennis said.

"Daughter?" Tina asked. "I thought he had a son."

"It turns out Ruth was William's daughter, not Norris's."

Johnny whistled. "That'll explain a lot."

"It might," Lesley said. She grabbed the Twix from her pocket and ate the second half of the stick she'd started on.

"There's also the thimbles," Dennis added.

"Thimbles?" Tina asked.

"Whittaker found a thimble in William's throat," Lesley said. "And last night, at Amanda's house, there was a thimble missing from a collection."

"So we think Amanda killed him?" Johnny asked.

"Not necessarily. She said no one else had been in the house in the last week, but that doesn't mean she or her husband can't have taken it before then."

"Or she could just be lying," Dennis suggested.

"Or she could just be lying, indeed," Lesley agreed.

"She said it was her mother's thimble collection," Dennis said, looking at the two constables.

"But she's senile, isn't she?" Johnny asked.

"That's what her husband told us," Lesley said. "But no one else has mentioned it, and we haven't seen the woman."

"You think *he's* lying?" Tina asked.

"I'm not sure what I think. But I want to know."

"Would she have wanted to kill William, if he turned up again after all these years?" Dennis asked.

Lesley shrugged. "He'd been gone for twelve years. Life had settled back down. It looks like they were all just going about their lives as if the truth about Ruth's parentage had never been uncovered."

Dennis nodded. "Then we need to go and see her."

"Yes." Lesley looked at Tina. "Anything else?"

"No."

"OK. The post-mortem is happening this morning. Can one of you two attend?"

Johnny looked at Tina, clearly waiting for her to volunteer. He was famously weak-stomached and had thrown up all the way across Poole Harbour when he and Lesley had worked a case on Brownsea Island.

"I'll go," Tina said, her voice heavy.

"Thanks." Next time, Lesley would tell Johnny to go. But she knew Tina would come back with a more accurate report, given that her focus would be on the PM itself and not on trying to keep the contents of her stomach inside.

She looked at Dennis. "Let's go see Mrs Coombs."

CHAPTER TEN

"I'M VERY SORRY, but Harriet isn't feeling at all well today."

"I'm sorry to hear that," Lesley told Norris. "But we have some questions that only she can answer."

"My wife has senile dementia. She won't remember anything."

Lesley knew that dementia sufferers could sometimes remember incidents from the distant past. William's disappearance was fairly distant, and the conception and birth of her daughters even more so.

"We won't stay long," she said. "If she becomes distressed, we'll leave."

He looked back at her, his nostrils flaring. "Five minutes. No more."

"Thank you."

Lesley and Dennis followed Norris into the house. Harriet was sitting in the conservatory, in a heavy chair facing the view of Ballard Down. There were fewer boxes this time.

"Harriet, love," Norris said. "I'm afraid that two of the

detectives want to speak to you. I told them you weren't feeling well enough, but they insisted."

She grunted. He bent towards her, holding his ear close to her lips. Lesley watched the side of the woman's face. How much was she aware of?

"If you're sure?" Norris muttered.

His wife nodded.

He pulled away. "She'll talk to you. But I'll be staying with her. She needs support."

A sound came from Harriet, almost a wail. Her husband bristled. "She's clearly not well enough."

Another wail. Lesley felt movement against her arm. Dennis was nudging her, gesturing towards Harriet. The woman had turned to look at Lesley, her eyes full of fear.

Lesley felt tension rise in her chest. "Mr Coombs, if you can leave us alone with your wife for five minutes, I promise we won't disturb her."

He looked between them and his wife. His cheeks were pale. "I'll be in the living room." The living room was right next door, separated from the conservatory only by thin glass doors.

Harriet grunted.

"Very well," Lesley told him. She lowered her voice. "Dennis, can you keep an eye on him?"

Norris left the room and positioned himself just beyond the glass doors. Dennis closed them, giving the man a grim smile.

Lesley sank to her knees, bringing her face close to Harriet's.

"Harriet?" she said. "Mrs Coombs?"

Lesley's phone buzzed. *Not now*, she thought.

CHAPTER TEN

Harriet nodded and turned to Lesley. A single tear ran down her cheek.

"Mrs Coombs? Is there something you want to tell me?"

Harriet glanced towards the doors. Dennis shifted position to place himself between her and her husband.

Lesley's phone buzzed again. She held it low so Harriet wouldn't spot it. The woman had closed her eyes.

Lesley flicked the text messages open. There was one from Gail: *Norris' prints on file from historical incident. Also found on outside of thimble. Not inside.*

If someone had used the thimble the way thimbles were supposed to be used, their prints would be on the inside. Norris might have handled it when helping his wife, or taking it to their daughter's house. But Lesley suspected not.

She looked at Harriet, who had her eyes squeezed shut. "Is it Norris?" Lesley asked, her voice low.

Harriet nodded, her head bowed.

"What has he done? Has he hurt you?"

A frown. Harriet rolled up her sleeve, her eyes still closed. There were needle marks.

Lesley pulled in a breath. "What is he giving you?"

"Don't know." It was barely more than a croak.

Shit. Lesley turned to Dennis. "Don't let him leave."

She turned back to Harriet. "Did Norris inject you?"

A nod.

"Did your doctor prescribe the drugs you were injected with?"

A shake.

"Do you think he killed his brother?"

Harriet squeezed her eyes shut. Another tear fell out. She nodded, her eyes closed and her body shaking.

"Do you use thimbles?"

Harriet's eyes opened wide. "I did," she whispered.

"Did you give them to your daughter, Amanda?"

Harriet looked puzzled. She nodded.

"And did Norris know you'd done that?"

Harriet grabbed Lesley's arm. "He took them to her."

Lesley swallowed the lump in her throat. Did they have enough to charge Norris?

She wasn't sure. But she did know that this woman was at risk, and she had to get Norris away from her.

She squeezed Harriet's arm. "We're going to keep you safe."

"Thank you."

Lesley stood up. She gestured for Dennis to open the glass doors. Dennis slipped inside the living room, his movements swift. He positioned himself by the door to the hallway.

Lesley stood in the conservatory doorway. She wondered if Harriet was watching or if she'd turned back to the view.

"Norris Coombs," she said. "I'm arresting you on suspicion of assault. You do not have to say anything..."

CHAPTER ELEVEN

Lesley shook herself out as she entered the main office. She still hadn't eaten, and last night she hadn't slept well. She was looking forward to Elsa returning.

Tina and Mike sat at their desks, their chairs pulled together so they were almost touching. As Lesley entered, Tina pulled her chair away.

Lesley smiled. "Feeling better now, Mike?"

"Sorry, boss. Sounds like I missed a murder investigation?"

"You did." Lesley looked at Tina. "Has Dennis filled you in?"

Tina nodded. "And we looked into Norris Coombs's past. Uniform were called out to the farm after a report that he was hitting Harriet nine years ago."

"After William disappeared?"

"A while after."

"Poor Harriet."

Dennis entered. "Uniform have brought Amanda Lloyd in."

Lesley turned to him. "Why?"

"She made a call to 999. Confessed to rearranging those thimbles for her father. She didn't know why he'd asked her to do it. But after we asked her about them, she was worried. She called him first thing this morning to ask him."

"She spoke to him before we got to the house?" Lesley asked.

"Yes."

He would have known they were onto him. Harriet had been so close to being in mortal danger.

Lesley scratched the itch on the back of her neck. "Good work, Dennis. We'll need to prepare for interviews with both of them."

"Yes."

The door opened and Johnny entered. Lesley clenched her fist.

"DC Chiles. Where have you been?"

"I went to the post-mortem."

"I asked Tina to do that."

"I volunteered. She's better at the data stuff than me."

Lesley unclenched her fist. "OK. And?"

"Whittaker is confident that William died of asphyxiation. There was water in his lungs but it hadn't got deep enough for drowning."

"Good work, Johnny." The DC had his moments.

She looked past him at Tina and Mike, who were giving each other furtive glances across the desks. When Tina spotted her, she gave Mike a meaningful look and quickly switched her attention to her screen. Lesley knew it hadn't been switched on yet.

"Good work, team," she said. "There'll be loose ends to tie up and forensics to collate. I'm hoping Gail can give us more on those thimbles. But I'm working on the assumption that William wanted to come home for good and Norris wouldn't allow that to happen. He'd made his life nice and cosy, tormenting his wife, drugging her, pretending nothing had happened and Ruth was his daughter. He probably lured his brother to the farm to kill him rather than risk bringing him to the house and anywhere near Harriet."

"A couple of potential eyewitnesses came forward last night, too," Johnny said. "I can go speak to them, if you want?"

"You do that. Take Tina too. And someone will need to speak to Tom Gains. The son. Looks like we'll have a fair bit to tell him after all."

Johnny nodded.

Lesley smiled. She beckoned to Dennis. "Let's do those interviews."

I hope you enjoyed reading *The Riverside Murder*. The next book in the series is *The Monument Murders*, which you can buy from book retailers or via my website.

Happy reading! Rachel McLean

DORSET CRIME BOOK 4, THE MONUMENT MURDERS

When a body is found draped over Swanage's iconic Globe monument, DCI Lesley Clarke is called in.

A message points to the motive: Go Home.

Is this a hate crime? Or something closer to home?

Lesley must find the killer before he or she strikes again, all while dealing with a mutiny in her team and political pressure from her boss.

At the same time, a local journalist has been investigating the death of Lesley's predecessor – and claims to have key information. Wary of involving her team, Lesley brings in her old colleague Zoe Finch to help.

Will Lesley come out of this case with her reputation, her team, and her career intact?

The Monument Murders is the fourth instalment in the bestselling Dorset Crime series, essential reading for everyone who loves Dorset... and gripping crime novels.

Buy *The Monument Murders* from book retailers or via the Rachel McLean website.

READ THE DORSET CRIME SERIES

The Corfe Castle Murders
The Clifftop Murders
The Island Murders
The Monument Murders
The Millionaire Murders
The Fossil Beach Murders
The Blue Pool Murders
The Lighthouse Murders
The Ghost Village Murders
The Poole Harbour Murders
…and more to come

Buy from book retailers or via the Rachel McLean website.

ALSO BY RACHEL MCLEAN

The DI Zoe Finch Series – buy from book retailers or via the Rachel McLean website.

Deadly Wishes

Deadly Choices

Deadly Desires

Deadly Terror

Deadly Reprisal

Deadly Fallout

Deadly Christmas

Deadly Origins, the FREE Zoe Finch prequel

The McBride & Tanner Series – Buy from book retailers or via the Rachel McLean website.

Blood and Money

Death and Poetry

Power and Treachery

Secrets and History

The Cumbria Crime Series by Rachel McLean and Joel Hames – Buy from book retailers or via the Rachel McLean website.

The Harbour

The Mine

The Cairn

The Barn

The Lake

The Wood

...and more to come

Read the London Cosy Mystery Series by Rachel McLean and Millie Ravensworth – Buy from book retailers or via the Rachel McLean website.

Death at Westminster

Death in the West End

Death at Tower Bridge

Death on the Thames

Death at St Paul's Cathedral

Death at Abbey Road

The Lyme Regis Women's Swimming Club series by Rachel McLean and Millie Ravensworth – buy from book retailers or via the Rachel McLean website.

The Lyme Regis Women's Swimming Club

...and more to come